my body

# my body meat

**Zak Ferguson**

*I have cut into my wrist and expanded the body meat into something far more cosmic than I had initially assumed such body mutilations could provide. I have broken down my pitiful performance artist guise into too many fragments, that I am, now, merely, human.*

*"I have failed as an artist, Mother."*

"How so?"

*"I sold a photograph of my latest performance for half a million dollars."*

"Well, that isn't anything to worry about."

*"Why?"*

"The hard dollar to the puffy pound is awful this time of year."

*"I am a sellout, aren't I?"*

"In what way, my love? You have struggled most of your life with finances and when you get seen get praised, get rewarded, and you witness the mammoth success of this empire you have built, might I remind you, which this arty thing is, it is your own empire, you have some existential crisis, not all over or about losing it all, but because you are making, what? Far too much?"

*"Yes"*

"Call me when you have a real-life issue, like being skint, you caught aids or whatever, you are pissing me off, Andrew."

*"Mother? Mum. Mama. Mamoi? Mummy?"*

*"What thoughts go through your mind during a performance?"* – this was a question asked by *Frénésie Artistique* resident cockblocker *Marshal El Rio* (only a cockblocker because he wanted me)/(not his real name)/(more of an office name)/(more of a stupid attempt at creating an image for himself)/(an image isn't important when you are a mere art critic/journalist)/(image and class and status is never acquired by the artist, as it is a continual reach for us, whereas the journos and critics don't even attempt a reach, they assume they have made it, and hence why they are not artists)/(they will never be the artists and shall remain as they are, *insignificant*, only **significant** in how they can boost and increase public relations, public appreciation, and exposure for the true artists in the making, for the artists in the phasing process, for the artist in the song and dance of their role as artist)/(these "men" and "woman" and shills will endlessly be caught in their own web of *want*, *desperation* and image-centric-lunacy - stuck in the mud as the image fashioner, spotlit, pointed at by the artists after they have sucked all life from them and what they can contribute to their career and exposure, who never will be)/(trapped as the questioner and never interviewee) - my response was,

my body meat

"Nothing."

"The moment is lost."

my body meat

"The body takes over."

my body meat

"Body overrides mind."

When in fact there is so much going on in my head I am surprised that each time I do not self-combust and reduce myself into a pitiful pile of human ash, sodden by the post-combustion tears that the elements captured before my bodily explosion.

I do.

I don't do.

I am.

I am not an am.

I am a thought moved onto a chess board and I devoid of all objectivity.

The objectivity is now the subjectivity bestowed to my pawn-body.

In mind there are words.

Bulletin points.

Bam.

Bang.

Smash cutting and layering over in a fleshy film with saturated colours that would make the likes of *Henri Georges Clouzot post*-Inferno proud, papa-handclapping and mother tear-jerking.

Ritual.

Rhythm.

Routine.

Separation.

You are you.

I am me.

Myself.

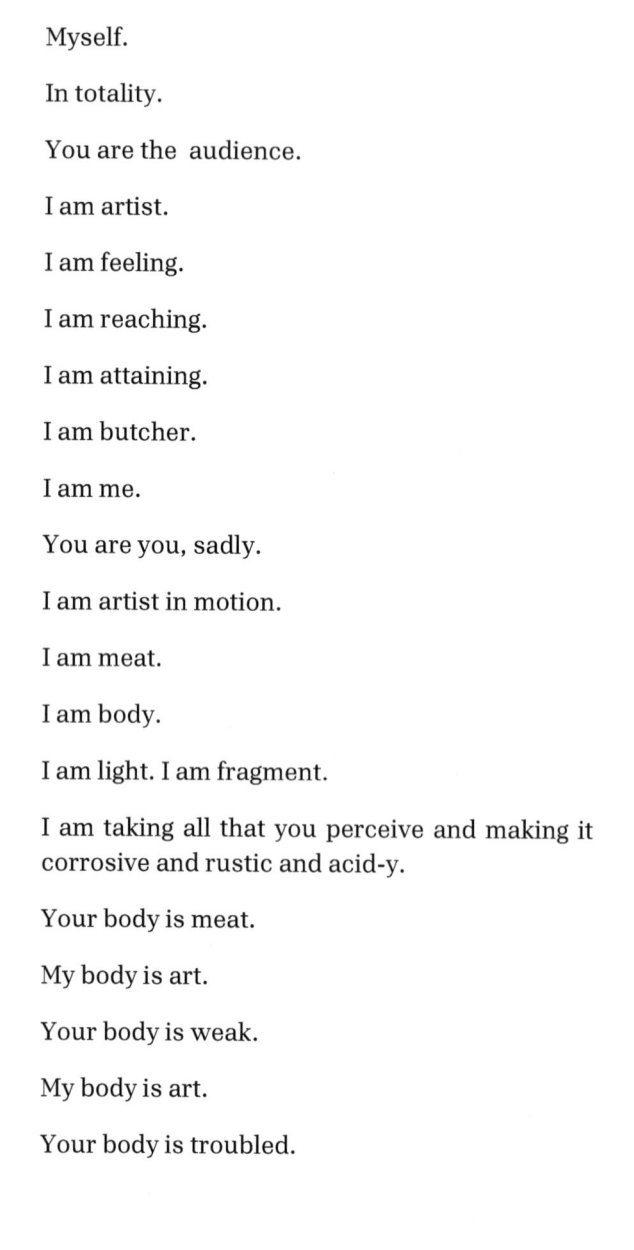

In totality.

You are the audience.

I am artist.

I am feeling.

I am reaching.

I am attaining.

I am butcher.

I am me.

You are you, sadly.

I am artist in motion.

I am meat.

I am body.

I am light. I am fragment.

I am taking all that you perceive and making it corrosive and rustic and acid-y.

Your body is meat.

My body is art.

Your body is weak.

My body is art.

Your body is troubled.

My body is art.

Your body is salted.

My body is art.

Your body is worthless in comparison to mine.

My body meat is paint, layered, thickened, cornflour added to.

My painted body is mixed in with dust and various studio provided muck and gruel.

I have the butcher's stench.

I am butcher.

I am the frame maker.

I have scars that are my own personal friezes.

Most friezes are personal, but I am unique in that I carry it around with me.

I pick the scabs of previous interviews.

I take the scab and chew it, playing with it, pressing against the back of the bottom row of my teeth.

I take the questions and I flip them, so they are laid out flat, and I rise their hips.

I expose the two-opposing (questions in the form of) arse cheeks and expose the glory hole.

I analyse them.

I obsess over them.

I dream of dreaming of a dreamer infiltrating the dreamland of the starfish vortex depthless endless succulent briny salty meaty texture and taste of the questioner's arsehole – his butt cheeks two question marks forced apart.


? ? - apart

O - the vortex and depthless and endless and meaty hole

?? - pressed together, so happy together.

These images come from the shared *id* of all the buffoons that read too much into my "art" when the truth is clear, in a transparent box - for all to preconfigure and to alter and to have the inner meaty truth be revealed to them post-coitus or midway through ejaculation; their seed; their vaginal juices shooting back up into themselves - in reverse - to sequester somewhere inside; whether womb or stomach lining for it to fester and be cut out and vomited over in response, highlighted on the medical spreadsheets as a sexual disease, a sexual infection, a sexual midway cum inversion caused by the realisation provided by me, protected in my transparent box, doing what I do, and loving what I do, ruining sex lives and later down the line people's sense of self and sexual promiscuity, and confusing the lines between sexual infection, old lovers and ending the third or first marriage because they have a secreted sexual disease. All because of me. The problematic issue is, they realise it is all a lark and thrust back at them, the sensation of a reverted cum-shot, takes precedence over the realisation I am mocking them, the general public and art gallery, art space, art appreciator.

*this is the truth*

*this is the scene*

*this is the moment*

*the words are useless*

*it is all dictated by my emotions*

*how my emotions respond to their reactions*

*this is the ambered fossil*

*this is the body*

*witness it undulate*

*witness the fractures*

*slow-mo this shit down*

*witness its end*

*witness its beginning*

*witness the crabby uncertain time in between*

*in the middle*

*the audience is enthralled to the corners of the sequences played out for them and in testament to a notion of them, them as audience and unwilling participants*

my body meat

I cut myself.

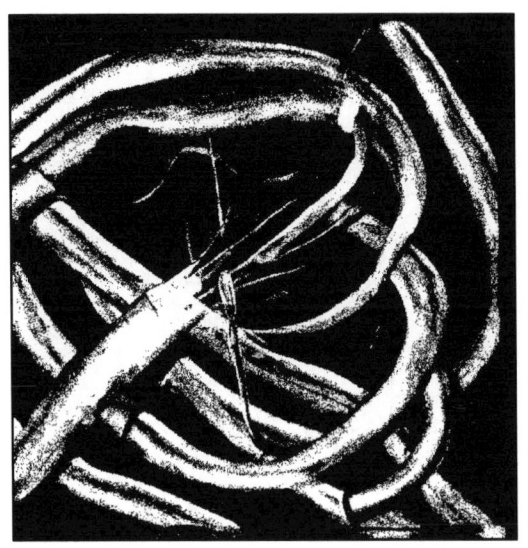

my body meat

This isn't a new thing.

my body meat

This is a new project.

my body meat

A new course of action.

my body meat

I cut deeper than I had ever before.

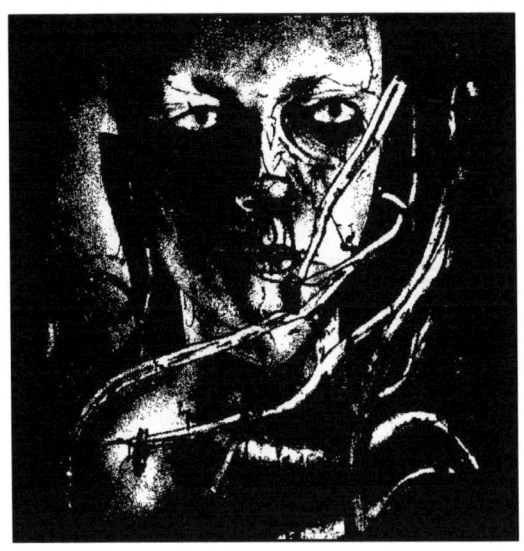

my body meat

It was not a slow incision.

my body meat

It was a full-bodied stab.

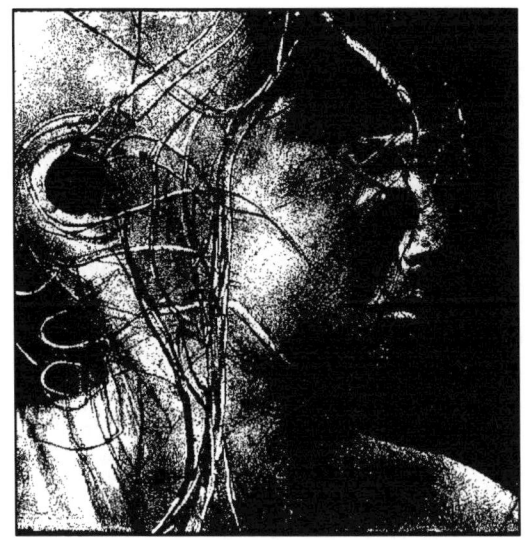

my body meat

I applied the pressure, the thrust, the plunge as I imagined all the serial killers I so admire via thriller-esque produced docs on Netflix (and... chill) would do/have done.

my body meat

I jerked the blade left, opening a nice chunky slice into and across my wrist.

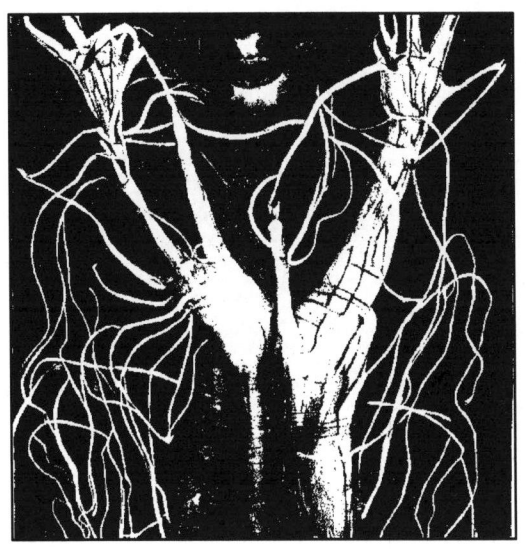

my body meat

*Deep.*

The tip of the carpet-cutter/Stanley knife (I have always preferred to refer to a SK as carpet-cutter, sue me, bitches!) and came up against a persistent pulsation.

my body meat

It shook the whole blade and hilt.

my body meat

It bumped up and down.

my body meat

Jarring the blade and the carpet-cutter's frame.

my body meat

The blood was not being forthcoming in its release.

my body meat

The artery was strong willed, I will give it that.

my body meat

I raised my wrist and the offending wound slashed across it up to eye level.

my body meat

I appreciated the line of blood that slowly forced its way up and around the blade, slowly moving downward, along the ridges and scars of previous body modifications and alterations and experiments.

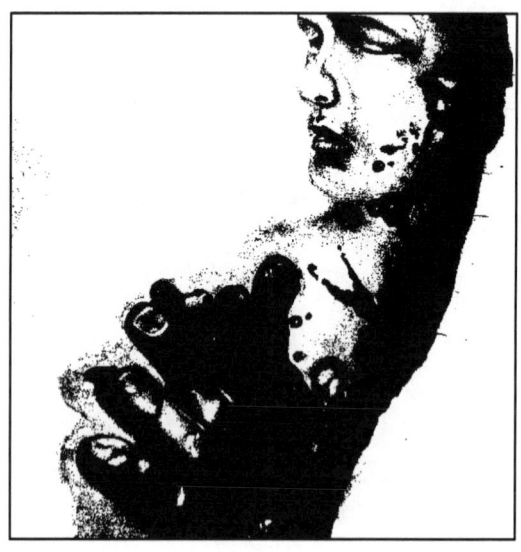

my body meat

The blood eventually dissipated into nothing.

my body meat

I could still feel the faint trace of invisible plasma crawling its way toward other sealed/healed exits/wounds' that its sibling rivulets of ruby-red had once escaped from.

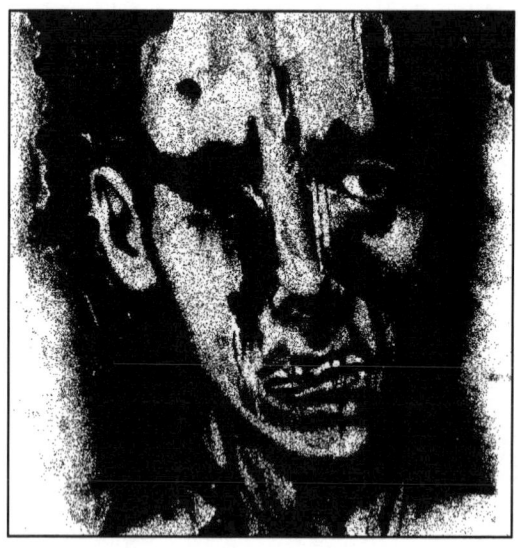

The blade seemed caught in the dip it had indented into the artery.

my body meat

It couldn't break through its tubular surface.

my body meat

I put more pressure down onto it.

The rest of the internal structure of my wrist seemed to be keeping their bloodied secrets, seeming opposed to this violent assault.

It wasn't new, this assault on my body with whatever sharp implement I could use to express and explore myself.

my body meat

This wrist, my left wrist, is virginal.

The tendons, sinews, internal flesh-materials were determined not to give up the plasmic ghost.

Blood was vital in the functions pertaining to the expression and the art of mutilation, in the act, in the various gestures and natural human responses that the body gives, and cannot quite stop itself from conveying/expressing/shaking through oneself; it gave the final hurray, it was a statement, it was lending to the unending obsession of mine; but, where was it?

It is that specific genetic code and biological necessity they do not oppose and bleat in protest over having to adhere to – the blood as lifeforms, amassed and cloistered as an armada.

The blood, the ingredient in one's life force, that keeps them bound to my interior self, was remaining elusive, and stubborn at best.

I revealed a universe, usually, but that day, it wasn't the blood flow from the artery I had set my mind on testing/tearing/carving into, it was the surrounding infrastructure and their minor leaks of krovvy.

my body meat

The shadows were abolished by my light pole – its effect weighing in on the scene/moment/confusing event.

my body meat

That cruel and revealing light beam.

my body meat

Creating harshness's where there shouldn't be any.

My manual strip tubing that I use in photographing myself, my pubes, my strange workspace, and its various corners, and dank isolated spots, was appeasing to a diseased mind like mine.

The last time I used this tube-lighting technique I employed a Nazi paraphernalia collector to bring along some of his cherished, and favourite of things for us to cause artistic chaos with.

my body meat

He did not disappoint.

As well as bringing two Nazi uniforms, that miraculously fit me as well, though both our heights and weights did not match, I got it into my pretty little grotesque mind that this is what he had been waiting for his whole entire life.

I created a fiction for us to perform, without the video cameras recording, without any form of audio equipment setup to capture our sighs, our reflective giggles, and supressed orgasms over doing something so *kitschy* and *vile*.

my body meat

We merely existed as **Nazi** and *Nazi*.

The strip light was wielded at one point by the both of us, tug of warring over this provider of sight and the dimensions created by the vast depths of darkness my studio space creates; but we were so conjoined, that of our intents and performances we merged, we were one Nazi package, so it seemed we were attacking not only each other, but that of ourselves with the tubing.

We made love with the uniforms on and I was left pleased that he encompassed the repressed German nations inherent pre 1950s homosexual urges/fetishes/denials.

my body meat

I was using it, this grand tubular glass tube, to light up the surfaces and the interiors of my wounds.

My mind wandered back into that stretched, elastic embrace where the British turned German turned kitschy turned sexual turned erotic turned erratic turned essential Nazi sympathiser and adorer, that when combined made one glorious spunky display.

The tendrils of experience wandering from my mind and that was escaping out of my ear and captured by the tube lighting as a detailed three-dimensional smoky display for me to either inhale or blow away – it gave over an odd religious fervour.

I was left admiring the released sexual tension, that would slowly come apart - my exhale would obliterate the fragment of sex, art, and cosmic unity – all by my own breathy volition.

I admired, but I didn't inhale as imagined and then I exhaled.

What has been presented as a facsimile of the past, needn't be re-experienced or re-processed.

my body meat

Do we all experience this at some point in our lives – the embrace of the one-time German collaborator - not lover – to see them disappear down the toilet?

I looked at the tube light, in my right hand, inspecting the tube, and looking through the cloudy glass, forcing the light to fuck up my vision – as I was inspecting the wound I was also blurring the vision of the moment/the fragment in time and not feeling as disturbed by the presence of unpredictability as I might have before in previous experiments unto my body meat.

That unique unpredictability afforded us body contortionists and obliterators, us bodily artists a sense of conviction   bestowed by our ambivalence and our insecurity and our reaches for the undiminishable power all man wishes to attain and mollycoddle into submission.

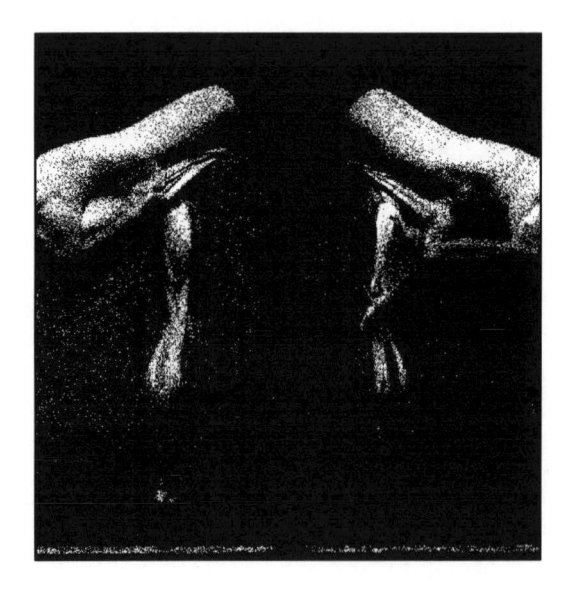

That unpredictability that such body mutilations often gush at a moment's notice where you are left deciding to bask in the outpouring of life, or just diminish it, and quench it.

my body meat

This has happened, far too often.

This tube light needed to be placed onto a stool
on the same level as my stretched-out arm.

A pole of not only light and what that means to this event and its artistic lending of sensation and obvious illumination... but it was also breathing its own sort of comfort to the scene/event/moment in non-time.

my body meat

A phallus lit up internally - providing external lighting permutations and phenomena.

It is an extension of the light sources I loathe too, but what is an artist without his particular rituals and tastes and opinions and contrarian backward and forwarding on his arty embodied self?

my body meat

I prefer blacked out rooms, with one source of light.

my body meat

It fits in with the melodrama of my pieces.

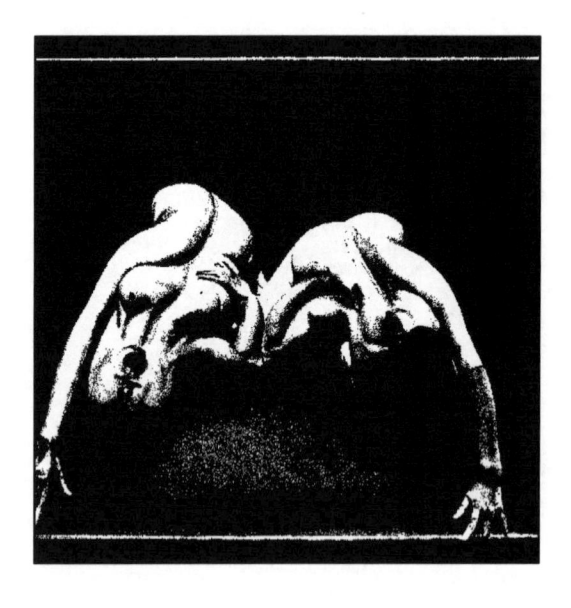

my body meat

Befitting my mind.

my body meat

Performance art is applied in everything I do.

Being in a five year relationship with a woman, convincing her I was just sex-shy as to the reasoning why I couldn't get it up, applying tender kisses and slopping clumsy licks to her clit to appease her, finger bashing her pelvis and bum hole, thumbing her anus, smearing myself, to keep her happy and enraptured and convinced, whilst I battled with the piece; *how long should it go on?*

What detriment will it have on her, and would I be able to forgive myself for never having completed it, in its full self as an art piece, if I pull out and make myself feel estranged, all so I couldn't witness the hurt I have caused.

my body meat

I likened it to a performance piece, one that is performed in secret; and I applied it to a gay closet performance piece I had written about in University – which was to great acclaim, but also judgement, warning me that this could be considered abusive.

my body meat

I waited for it all to unravel.

For it to... Reveal itself to me, instead of poking at it and hoping it would pop.

my body meat

The truth was I was not performing in a performative way but a detrimental way.

my body meat

I was lying to myself.

my body meat

*Fuck her,* she was never important.

my body meat

What **was** important was the life lessons I learned.

my body meat

Women are boring after a while.

my body meat

Men are hot.

my body meat

I am not.

my body meat

I need to exile myself before my ugliness does damage to the few good men left in my sordid little London based world.

my body meat

I had fought with the blade and the artery for two hours, and still nothing wished to be expressed.

my body meat

I decided to give it up.

my body meat

I pressed the two-opposing skin-lines back together, and before I could apply my own stiches and medical glue (I have contacts, darlings) it sealed itself up.

Before it finally resolved itself back into its all natural and original surface, a clear, undamaged and intact wrist... I noticed a translucency beneath a corner of both the different sides of the split skin... and it was almost positioned and divinely sectored at the edges of both sides of the open wound; one that seemed produced by a warm glow, much like my tubular glass lighting-strip – trapped beneath my skin.

my body meat

Before I could come to terms with this ardent illumination from within, it started to slowly fade out, sensuously, and in some whacked out religious style.

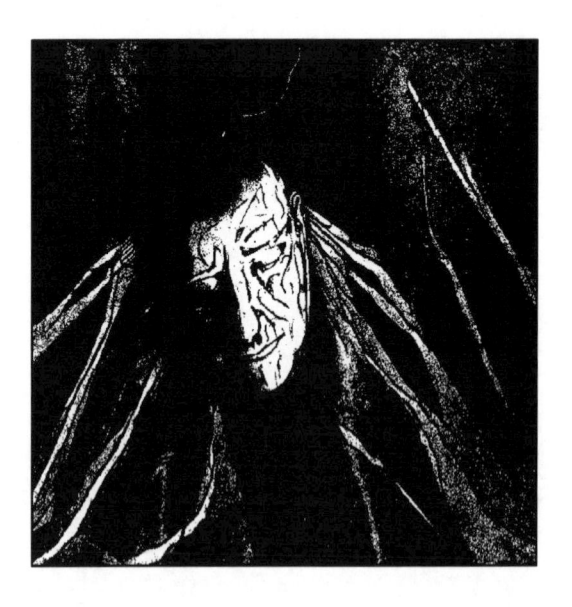

my body meat

The experience was processed in dreams.

In these dreams there was a soft glow, much like the soft, warm glow emanating beneath my conjoining skin flaps.

my body meat

My hands were tubular.

They were viscerally taking on the viscera of the mind's assumption of what the wound could have provided if I managed to cut into that reinforced and armoured carapace that decided to instigate a process I cannot fathom, into protecting my left wrist's artery.

my body meat

My hands branched out.

The tubular trunks, the vascular worms climbed, progressively getting swollen, though firm, they took on the waviness of succulent underwater plants.

They bent, they curved, they undulated, they did all the things that aquatic plant life does to keep themselves entertained and revivified.

my body meat

My hands and the wounds turned each other inside and out that it no longer resembled a hand with a wound or a wrist with a hand attached to it.

my body meat

It was a thick paint, applied to the canvas called *the cosmos.*

my body meat

There were corrals situated in the bloody depth of my healed wound.

my body meat

My hand was both lit and lightening up the perverse quarantined zone it was sequestered within.

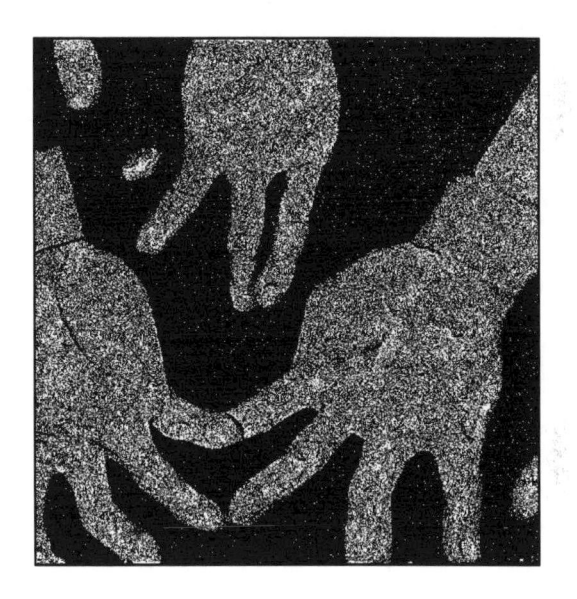

my body meat

I picked up my phone and scrolled through my list of contacts until I find the only one who could help me with this current project.

my body meat

I messaged him, the weirdly spaced-toothed ex-lover of mine.

my body meat

His swollen face and parted rubbery lips, it made me swan head over cracked heels, as they accentuated the tombstone teeth of his.

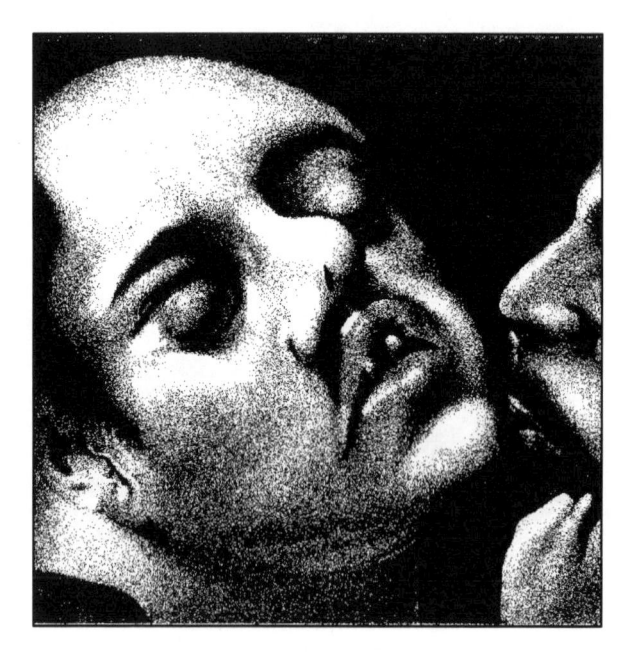

"hello"

"hello"

"who is this"

"me"

"oh, it is you"

"how did you know"

"you are the only egotistical person I know who thinks by stating me is enough for the other person on the other end of the phone to go, oh, yeah, it is you, it is all elementary, and also ego driven, you are the only bloke I know who will answer with me, as if that is validation enough for somebody that you know on the other end who might not know you to snap out of reality and go…"

"shut up you are boring me already"

"what do you want"

"i am in the midst of a discovery"

"midst"

"within it"

"that isn't a really a discovery, it is already discovered, isn't it" "you make no sense, also three conversation lines back you prattled on and on, and I am now questioning why I chose you"

"for what"

"to dramatize the unfolding event I have managed to create for myself"

"you cut yourself up again and want someone to plead with you, do not do it, your body cannot cope, what about infections, when I have already spent too much of my time doing such a thing, so the answer is a simple…"

my body meat

He put the phone down on me.

my body meat

Sometimes I really should just let people be, because when I introduce humanity into my work, it gets messy, all because the mess is always integral to the (previous) pieces in question, because it is a contradiction upon a contradiction, and even calling up a person is sacrilegious to my current preoccupation with total social ostracism.

I imagine knocking his teeth out and him just laughing as his tooth flies out of his mush in slow motion whilst we ourselves are totally out of sync with this slow-time performance piece.

my body meat

# What a bitch!

my body meat

He put the phone down on me.

my body meat

He ended the call.

my body meat

What a beautiful soul.

my body meat

He may be fat, and he may be stupid on an aesthetical and exterior level, but he always knew how to mindfuck and fragment my methodology.

my body meat

That is why I am still in love with him.

These types of conversations were what really grounded me.

my body meat

Being a performance artist, with so many grants coming out my backside and the various teaching gigs and scholarships created in my name, I had too much money, sometimes too much spare time, and I filled in the gaps with mental games, abuse, intolerance, self-centred melodramas.

my body meat

Life is a performance in of itself.

I just get paid to do it.

my body meat

my body meat

I do it in as many ways and guises as I can; if I have some result; whether photographs, performances, video-performances, video-projects, art of all mediums – put out to make me proud, and to make me absurdly richer, then, three cheers for me, *hip-hip-hooray, hip-hip-hooray, hip-fucking-hip-hooray!*

my body meat

I do all of them – all those previous mentioned mediums, very well.

My healed wound was concerning me, the more that I allowed myself to frame the previous evenings occurrences.

The wound needed to be reopened. Had it ever been a wound? It necessitated an exploration. It needed to be opened up, anew, as if that spot hadn't ever afflicted by my carpet-cutter tool - as it bared no markings, or my favourite thing about bodily performative mutilation, is the minor inflections left on the body. I focused on the wrist. It was virginal. Untouched. Nothing to indicate I had stabbed it with a Stanley knife.

my body meat

My scars represent my commitment to the artform of body distortions and experimentation.

My body usually maintains all the distress I have visited upon it.

The body is meat.

It marinates with each physical allusion and impression pushed into its amorphous bulk.

My body meat is there for me to carve, to scarify, to test, to push beyond its limits.

my body meat

Infections are a reward.

my body meat

My body has been commercialised.

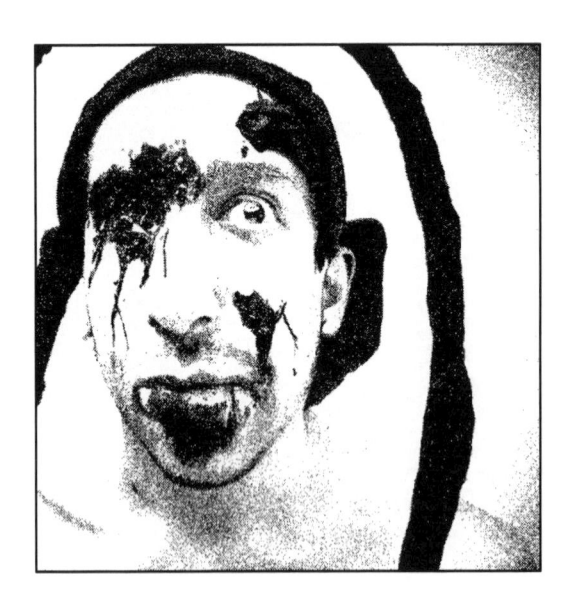

The wound smiles often because it has nothing else to do but smile; and eventually a smile forms into a wry grin, afforded weight, and a reality by the serrated skin, that has scabbed over, that the sentient wound uses as its toothy tissues to provide its lewd grin.

my body meat

Can a grin ever be lascivious or lewd or crude or libidinous?

my body meat

My wounds can.

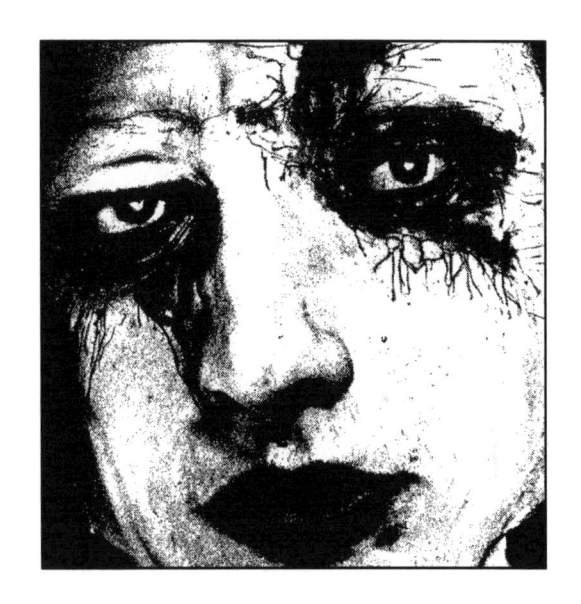

My avant-garde, transgressions have been granted finances, awards, patron cash flow, appreciation, praise, rants, gesticulations that form the body language of the neanderthals.

my body meat

I am given various avenues to move into and explore and yet I am still trapped in this tawny encasing to keep myself going.

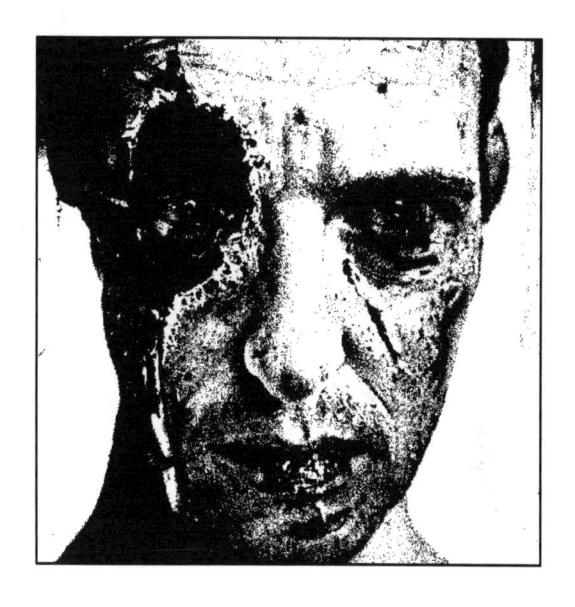

It is an encouragement to mutilate and self-harm.

The self-harm we all at some points have considered and attempted is embodied and various sampled and delivered by my dear meaty self.

my body meat

I am to be the avatar for all those who believe this body meat of mine is put out on display for brutalization and deep cuts, a death by a million (fuck a thousand) cuts.

My body meat is my audience's body.

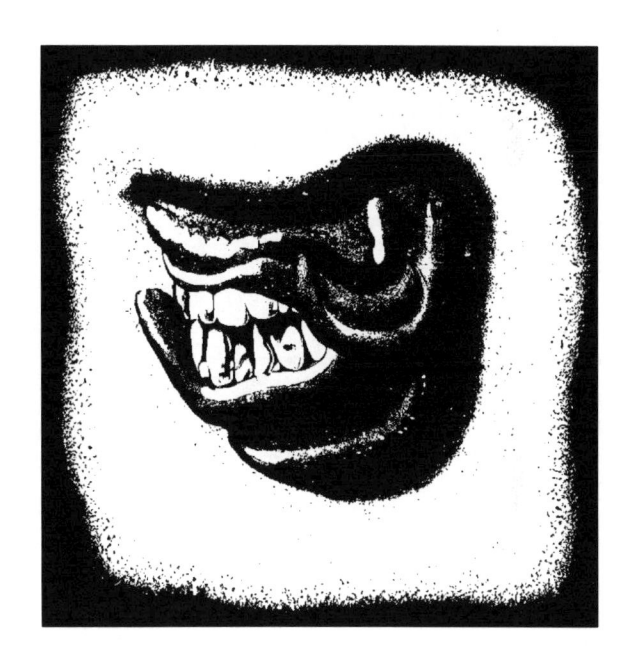

There is a shared mania, witnessing performance pieces created by the body itself and the commander of said body.

It is an unabating pulsation of awe, wonder, disgust, and admiration.

my body meat

Humans love to be shocked.

my body meat

I shock.

my body meat

I love to shock.

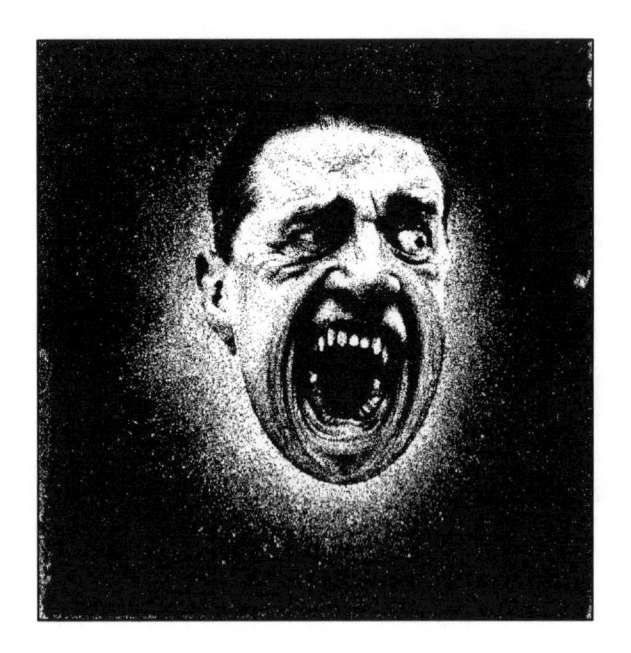

my body meat

I am the shock in meaty form.

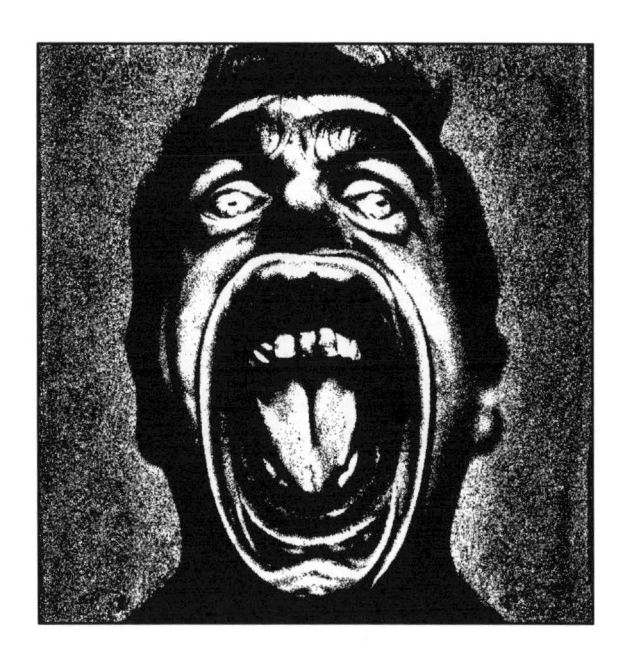

my body meat

I also transcend the means of said shock by capturing my various body mutilations in different, yet as ever accepted mediums.

my body meat

I cater and I adhere.

I have made the underground grunge popular and sophisticated, enough to earn dollars, euros, and various incomes with my various videos, photographs, presentations, and poetic musings.

my body meat

Mere meat with various complexes that keep it running.

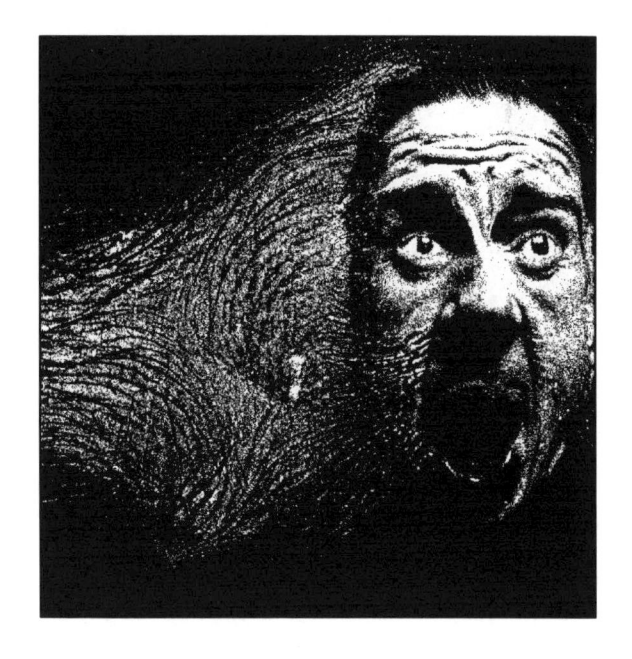

The brain does too much and too little and the *id* of oneself does the rest.

I am outside of the brain and all the various mental-electric-volts that makes a little toe wiggle, and a penis wilt under the pressure of consummating something that we are told evolution does not wish for us to do.

I left my studio, a deadly sin in my ritual, but I had to get out. I didn't pay attention to what I looked like.

I only came to, out of this desperate need to get some fresh air, some communication between me and what lives on beyond my studio.

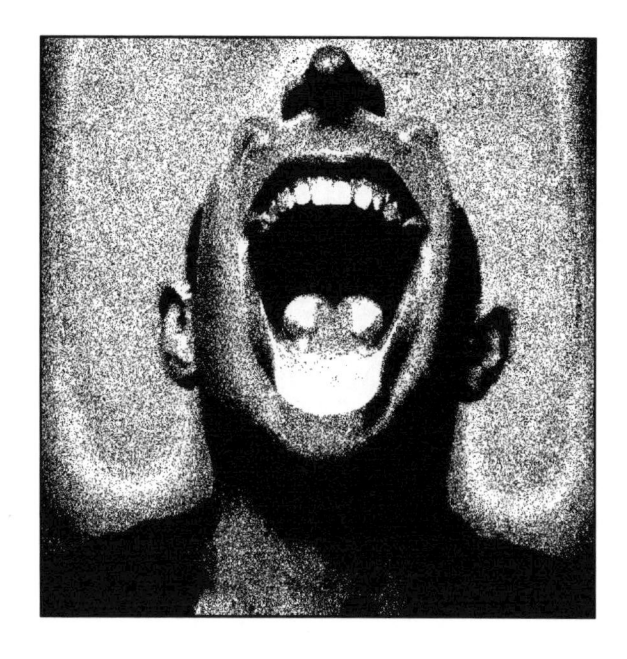

my body meat

I broke the so-called fever within minutes and gathered myself.

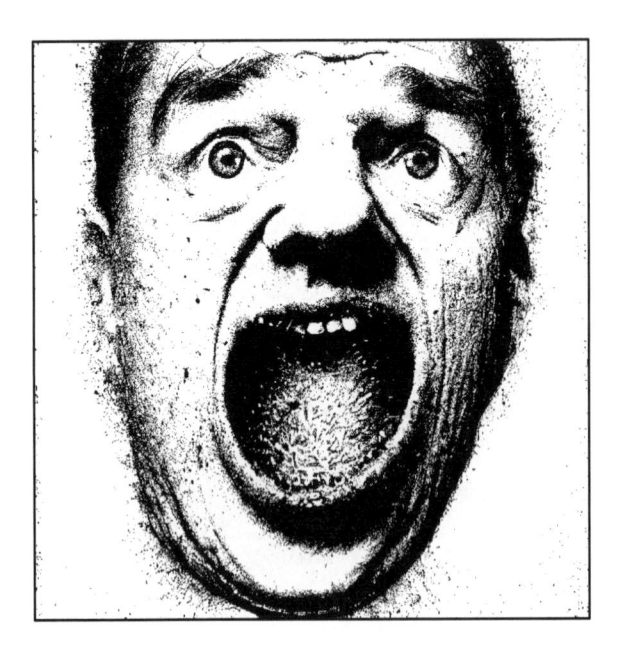

I decided to neglect that fact that I was half naked, yes, but again, what else do people expect in this artsy fartsy avenue?

I started pressing buzzers, all of them, and laughed as a few answered lickety-split, the bored artists like me, perhaps on the ledge of inanity, needing a push to get away from their artistic spaces, and not the work, never the work – cancelling out the other.

Flat 6 answered first, the voice taking on the neediness such artists put unto themselves, crying in their lonely messy corners, encouraging some sympathy out of strangers via intercom.

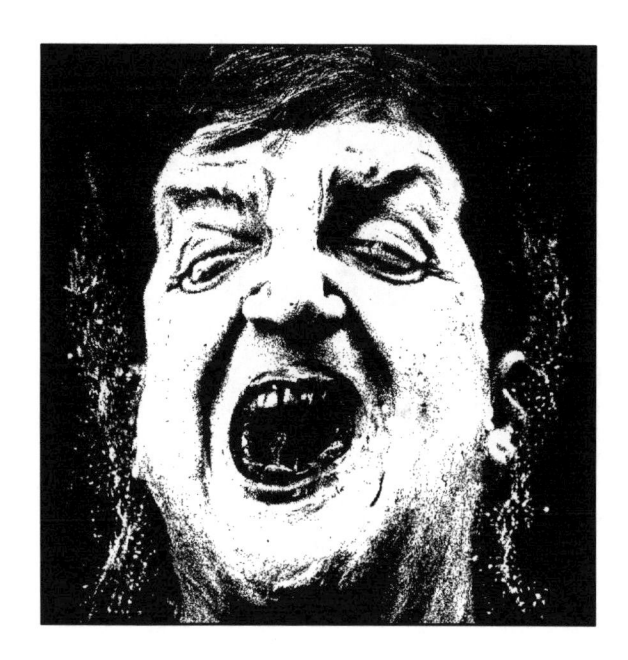

my body meat

Then Flat 12 answered, cutting over Flat 6, whose neediness was obliterated and replaced by desperation.

my body meat

Flat 6 started piping up louder, trying to talk over Flat 12.

my body meat

I left them to it, arguing between themselves.

I skipped on merrily and decided to head away from the apartment blocks and converted buildings to more homely neighbourhoods and initiated my not so dedicated game of knock-knock-ginger.

my body meat

Where the knock failed, I pressed the brass buttons, or pulled the lavish knotted cords.

my body meat

I even got some gumption and leaned out from
the concrete steps and tapped the glass.

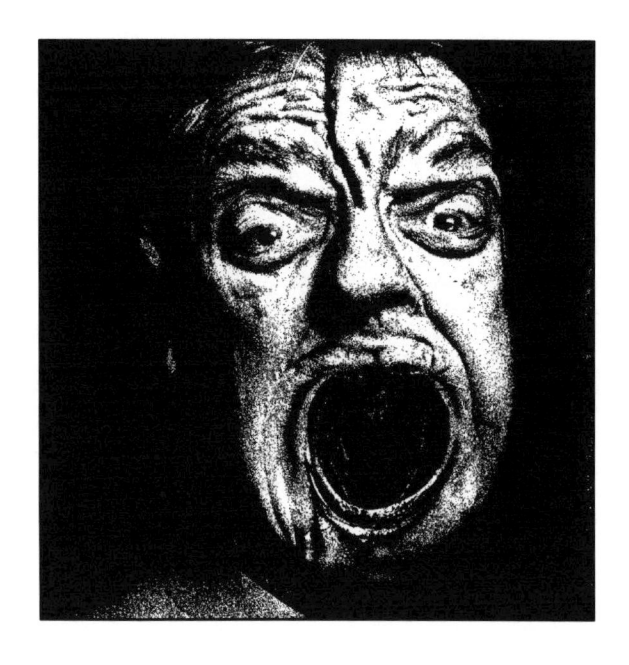

Nobody answered or seemed willing to come answer.

A few left parcels indicated they were either out or the types that slept in until the afternoon.

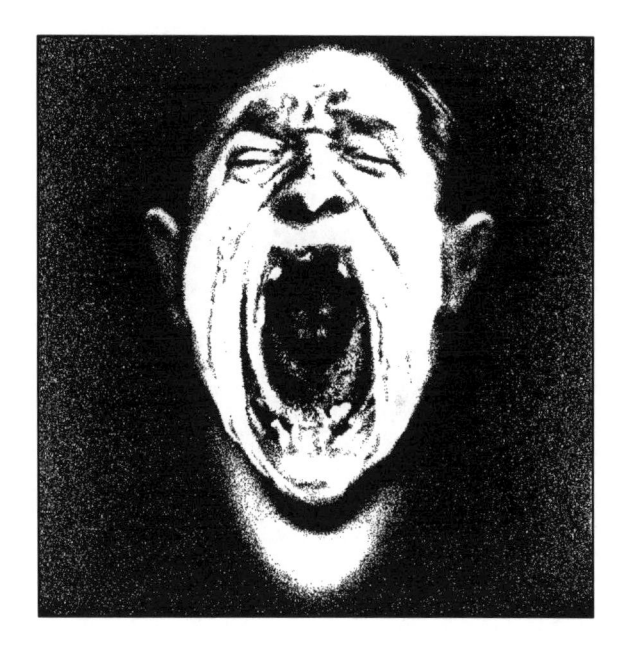

my body meat

A couple of doors that I tapped on the front windows eventually opened, but that was when I had given up, focused on the next doors to knock.

As I knocked on various doors I morphed it into another game, an experiment.

my body meat

I wanted to knock on doors with that oak finish effect.

When that resulted in a dear old heart who had an absurd shadow cast behind her, I couldn't help but envision the reaper man was following her out, finally given time to take advantage of her sudden silence, moving in edgeways, conversation wise, finally given enough time to raise his scythe and cancel her earthly life out. It unnerved me, so I made my apologies, still not totally aware that her slack jaw wasn't the reaction to the first pierce of the reaper man's blade (a few oldies need a couple of swipes and slashes to cut them from this material plain) but shocked at my naked self, and the state I was in. That later houses I had picked were giving off bad vibes. I could hear the enquiring, "What?" and the Where's? and the Why's? and the "Stop knock-knock gingering me you little bastards!" as I made my hastening-self disappear from their doorsteps, and lives. I stumbled across a rather fetching door, that was a mere street away from my studio; I think I was meaning to go back home, to do whatever it was I was doing - done with my little adventure town ward. I again lost track of both body movement, place, and my intent. This door, from what I can recollect, was down the road, around a corner, provided by a sly alleyway, the best of all alleyways. They give of a creeping sense of dread and potential harm. Secreting yobos, vile youths, or pass their sell by date cruisers. The most perfect of corners this alleyway had, the concealing corner - that transitioned from cracked, stained paving stones to cobblestones, featuring a variety in different states of decay and rootedness; some that rattled and quaked under your foot and others that remained rooted and affirmed in their cemented place. A beautiful circular path leading you around this cul-de-sac of grand, mansion-esque houses. I waddled up this sweet, shockingly well veiled cobblestoned cul-de-sac and I knocked on the first door I came upon. Nobody answered. By the tenth door I noticed the fetching door. Oak finish, brass cornices, and a beautiful stained-glass window. Through the stained-glass pane set into the front door - the geometric patterns warping the person that was coming to receive me – but not warped or distorted not enough to put me off from instigating a conversation – I waited as they took their time unlocking the door. I appreciated the drag, the creak, the rusty permutations offered by the noise of the locks and deadbolts being unleashed. The man revealed himself, and I was not disappointed. Middle aged... Maybe older. I'd have said mid-fifties, in a frayed cardigan, wearing loafer slippers, a bald pate, and teeth threatening to fall out of his head, one by one, like weeds that unroot themselves. "Sir, please could I use your bathroom?" I asked. "Your covered in blood!" he replied, looking me up, and down, and then up and down again, as if to try and indicate to me that how I was displaying myself needed to be taken in consideration. "It is my work, please, I really need to disinfect..."

"What you done?" he started, interrupting me, and before I could go into details, not knowing fully where this was going, whether I needed to do what I had begun to tell him I needed to do, he just went into, not a rage, but a prolonged uninterrupted fragmented spiel of confusion, questions, and paranoia. "Who are you why are you what are you doing knocking on my door is that your blood or somebody else's and also why you smiling at me or why you holding onto your oh by Jove you are indeed stark bleeding naked I do not know this seems all suspect then again if you wanted to mug me you wouldn't mug me you would try to fuck me not that I think all faggots want me but you are slimy with blood and if we wrestle like in that Ken Russell movie I would be the victor and I wouldn't nor couldn't call you the spoils and do you need the bathroom specifically or do you need just a sink I don't make it a thing letting naked blood splattered strangers into my humble abode but you look queenie enough to be safe and I ain't no homophobe but I gotta try figure out if you are a flight risk or an old Bernard Williams Sharath house risk, you understand me kid? Kid? Kid? Why you walking away?"

I gave up. I left. I got back home and tried to compile all that I had experienced and done, and the whys. A few hours later I still couldn't come up with anything. I again went through my contacts on my phone, and randomly selected someone and waited for them to answer the call.

He/she/they/them/the world over didn't answer. I was left alone. I looked at the offensive extension that would not be made malleable and artistic – my left wrist – and began slamming it into different surfaces. I wanted it to crack like chinaware. I wanted it to fissure and reveal the glow I had seen the day before. I needed the unreality of the moment to consolidate the artistic impressions I slap on everything related to my actions, motions, thoughts, gestures, experiments, self-harming. I wanted to be a sculpture in the figurine forms of Giacometti, gathering smut and pornographic desire. I wanted to be Kevin Bacon, only a little shorter, gasping for breath, struggling to recreate my *Foot Loose* moves, as William S. Burroughs stood on the sidelines, a gorgeous spotlight illuminating his deeply wrinkled face, the keep trenches in that face hiding phrases he was at that time ill-equipped to use and rephrase into his sludge pile of genius, as he cocks a shotgun, allowed a faint trace of a smile, a smile he last had to hide from the general public since September 6th, 1951 – slowly etching a new facial structure, smoothing out the creases, words and letters dropping, where that smile, faint, hardly ever witnessed was allowed to creep back into his wry self. Kevin Bacon as a morbidly obese man. Kevin Bacon as Freddy Krueger. Kevin bacon as painted by Francis Bacon. The foot loose, oh the foot loose, steps, pirouettes, the choreography that bound him and Kyra Sedgwick together, forever more taking control of my body. I am a framer, and the art is nothing, as I am the framer and the framer needs to construct a frame that betters, improves, enhances the art in question. Who is my framer? Where has this gone. I have mood swings. I have lovers. I fuck to feel and feel so I can attempt to fuck. I have a wrist that will not be broken, sliced, and torn open to give me that sensational glow, that it had done before. I look at my drug pile, my weirdly totemic pile, that I use, abuse, cut up, grind, roll, inhale, never inject, and all it affords is a breakdown of my schizophrenia into fragments to better surmise their origins. I flail. I hit. I destroy. I wanted my arm to be given a new lease of life. The blood didn't spray or splatter or taint my white curtains and crème-coloured walls – the lights didn't discharge religious illuminati approved lighting striations to this scene. This scene ends as it started. I have cut into my wrist and expanded the body meat into something far more cosmic than I had initially assumed such body mutilations could provide. Then it reverts into a thought. Thought reverts into a time capsule, a nodule in the back of the artistic stratum. I have broken down my pitiful performance and artist guise into too many fragments, that I am, now, merely, human. I am now merely benign. I am now merely creating a mythology for myself. The reality dawns. I am not an artist. I am a sad pathetic poof with too many projects and not enough will power to take the reins of these subjects, these materials, all provided by my body, and put them on hold. Like my lovers, my exes do with every call. I have imagined so many conversations that end with, "I love you too, but you are too extreme." And I am not even given that type of levity. They all say the same thing, "You are going to kill yourself." The list goes on and I sample them. "You want to harm yourself, and as excuse have made a career out of it, and the only end result is permanent disfigurement or death." I want to hear something unrelated. That is my own fault. My work is my life. My art life is my life. There are no interchangeable markers, not anymore. I am body. I am meat. My body meat is there for the taking. The glares, the stares, the shock, is it enough? Shock and ridicule birthed from my own actions and examples rather than allowing people to break me down into their biased component parts. I am clown. I am artist. I am performer. I am my own bloody worst meat factory. The body continues and thrives under these assaults. "What is too much? Only you know that, and for me, the first two experiences of witnessing your absurd body mangling, that was too much." When is enough ever enough. I am greedy for exposure. I am horny for praise. I am also a slut for punishment. The body, the harm, the physical and nerve-end sizzling responses I can take have become numb-sensations. It is the exterior affectations and effects my art creates that bolster, bullies, harangues me. I need to do this all so I can feel. Let me feel. Let me harm myself. Death will not be the release. The release will be when my true loves realise that I do what I do because there is nothing else that I can do to exact this hidden crumb of affection. I am brutally honest, scathing, in tongue waggles and hip thrusts and medium meat penetrations because the body is immaterial. It is the emotions I need. I want. I have to tell the truth through my art. Through my existence put on display. There is little to no thrill. It is all garbage. I am the way I am, so somebody finally reveals the core of the performance and body mutilations; I am looking for my one true love. I am meat. I am bone. I am art. I am throne. I am heat from your thighs. I am semen flying in arcs to dissipate into nothing. I am my body. I am my meat. I am a tool. I am a guise. I am a mask. I am a thousand cuts delivered onto the left virginal wrist. I have nothing and everything. Money means nothing. Body meat means brutality. Body means self. Body means aggravation. Body means disintegration. Body meat goes to rot. My body is the meat of the world, of the universe. My body meat is now no longer yours, ours, or mine. It has been proffered to a higher entity in supplication, and in honour of feeling something other than guilt and shame. I am not an artist. I am a fictional character. I am not a fictional character I am merely animal protein. I am honestly nothing without you, whomever you are. I got shot in the arm once for a performance and I pressed both thumb and forefinger into it. I pinched nerves, I wiggled the interior mess. Still, I felt nothing. Nothing translated as void. The body is put through so much and as much as we adhere to strict regimes and diets and follow the latest trends it is all for nothing. We are all meat and will all rot, or be burned to ashes, or left in some coffin in some graveyard with some worms doing their warmish things, and the maggots haven't set in yet, but that's okay, as we are not getting out of this predicament. The body reminds us that there is nothing spiritual. We are all body and no soul. We are all but meat. We have been fed, guided, pushed, dragged, pitted, and thrust into existence to know that life isn't special or specific. It is what it is. You are here. Then you are not here. Why was I trying to transcend when my mutilations answered the immortal question concerning mortality. We are meat. And will forever be seen and processed as meat. Meat isn't emotional. It is biological. Meat isn't artistic, it is frail. My body meat and all that I have endured and created out of some wanky sense of deification is a lie. Our bodies are grown to rot. We rot early, sometimes, or we rot late. It is still the same process. We are meat. My art is making a point that, though you witness the transcendental, the whimsicality of the performance, and you frame it in whatever materials you have acquired in your lives, meaning your life experiences, and those events that shape you, all so you can equate and define, and individuate, it is pathetic and wrong. It is fruitless. This isn't art. It is farce. This farce is the reality of body. The reality of our souls, which are just fanciful names/notions and fictionalisations to make us feel important and in a position to poeticise and romanticise all so we cling onto the concept that when the body leaks, oozes, explodes, comes apart over time or in a tragic accident, the form of our identity and sense of place and our self, our own glorious masterfully fucked up selves, it is a long game, a long hustle and shared delusion. It is put in place because we cannot accept the exceptions of reality, being that we are all meat packages passing ourselves off in whatever fashion we like in hope we leave a mark, a stain, an imprint. We all rot. We all rot, and we are all but meat somehow in a position to fuck, feel and transmit various flesh-pulsations. It is disorienting. It is a fiction we all feed into. Our bodies are not there to cherish and abuse. That is already something that is destined for us before we are a mere twinkle in your horny Father's youthful, or not so youthful, aged eye. My body meat is meat. Nothing else. It is not art. It is not a tool. By doing this for so long, I have made myself into a fool. Witness me. Look upon my legacy. My art. And weep, weep for me, and the future generations when they realise that we are nothing but fucking pathetic meat sacks. My body meat unto yours.

my body meat

# my body meat

# About the Author

Zak Ferguson is an experimetnal author/writer & director/noise-maker. He lives in Brighton, UK.

Rumour has it he is quite an amiable chap.

Rumour also has it that he is a bit of a twat.

my body meat

Copyright 2023 ©

Copyright 2023 © Sweat Drenched Press

Cover art/Interior Art by Zak Ferguson

ISBN: 9798872235521

This book or any portion thereof may not be reproduced or used in any manner whatsoever without the express written permission of the publisher or writer except for the use of brief quotations in a book review or article.

All rights reserved.

my body meat

I know i went way
over the top with the
Dennis Cooper blurb!